UNCLE WIZZMO'S NEW USED CAR

UNCLE WIZZMO'S NEW USED CAR

BY RODNEY A. GREENBLAT

Harper & Row, Publishers

Library of Congress Cataloging-in-Publication Data
Greenblat, Rodney Alan, 1960–
    Uncle Wizzmo's new used car / by Rodney Alan Greenblat.
       p.   cm.
    Summary: Uncle Wizzmo makes his annual trip to Turnpike Larry's to
pick out a new used car.
    ISBN 0-06-022097-X : $. — ISBN 0-06-022098-8 (lib.
bdg.) : $
    [1. Uncles—Fiction.   2. Automobiles—Fiction.   3. Humorous
stories.]   I. Title.   89-36577
PZ7.G8277Un 1990   CIP
[E]—dc20   AC

10 9 8 7 6 5 4 3 2 1

First Edition

Dedicated to John Gandert and Albert Greenblat,
my grandfathers.

Every spring Uncle Wizzmo goes out to buy
a new used car, and we go with him!

It's a long drive from our house to Fleeberville.

We wave at the animals on Mrs. Nickels' farm.

We drive past Goose Lake and Snookersburg,

past the windmill and the recycling plant.

We stop for french fries at Burgerworld,

then on to Fleeberville!

Fleeberville! What a place!
Signs and shops, motels and restaurants!

We stop at the red light.
The used car lot is just ahead.

Every spring Uncle Wizzmo visits
Turnpike Larry's used car lot.

Turnpike Larry is always happy to see Uncle Wizzmo.

Turnpike Larry is a friendly sort of guy.
He shakes our hands and gives out
free hot dogs and soda.

Then he starts showing us the cars.

Some of the cars are ugly.

Some of them are old.

Some only need a paint job.

RUNS GREAT!

Some have too much paint.

ONLY ONE OWNER

This one looks like a turtle.

This one looks like a bowl of fruit.

This one looks like a bunny.

'72 FLUFFY (AUTOMATIC)

We don't know what this one looks like.

'99 GOGOMOBILE

"Only driven once!" says Turnpike Larry.

But it's way too big.

This one is just too much!

What about this one?

We always stop for ice cream on the way back home.
"I love ice cream!" says Uncle Wizzmo.

And away we go in Uncle Wizzmo's new used car.

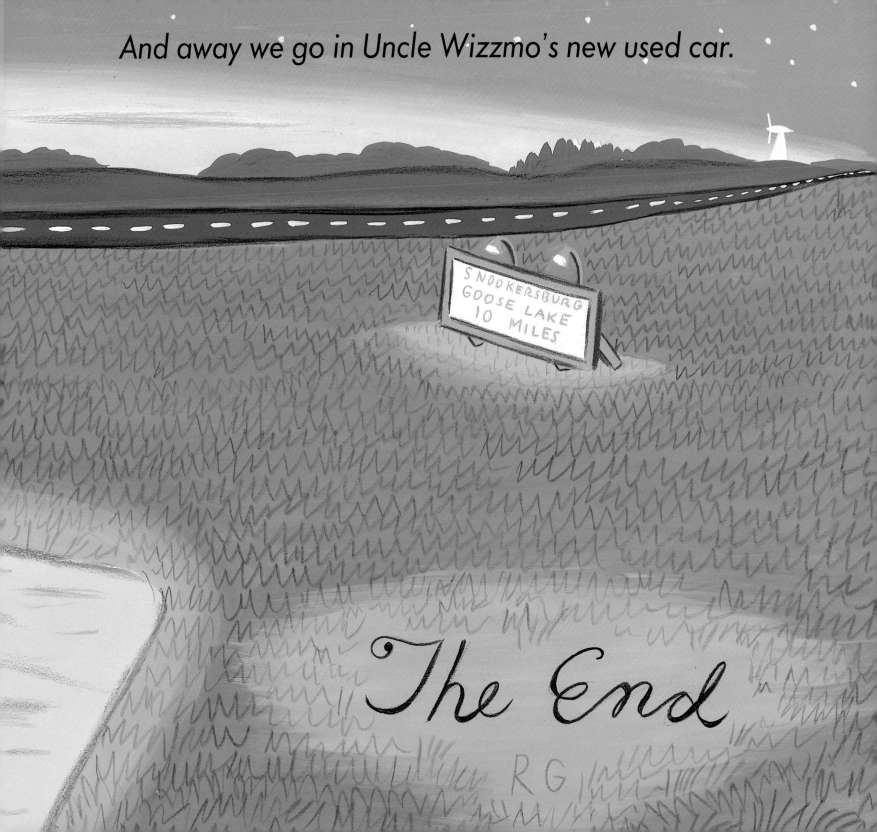

SNOOKERSBURG
GOOSE LAKE
10 MILES

The End

RG